Richard Torrey

WHY?

HARPER
An Imprint of HarperCollinsPublishers

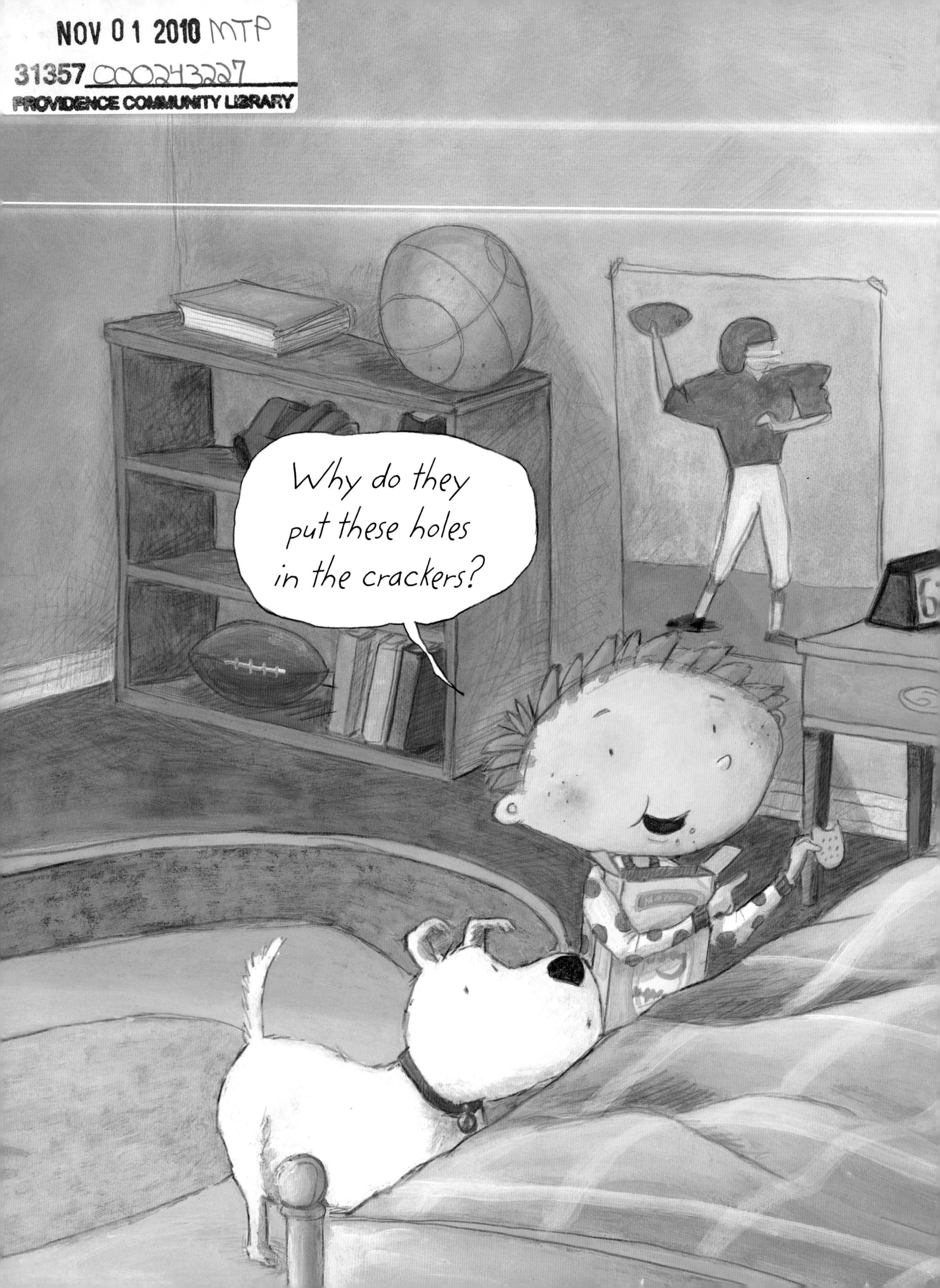
Why do they put these holes in the crackers?

Why do feet stink?

Why does all the good-for-you food taste bad?

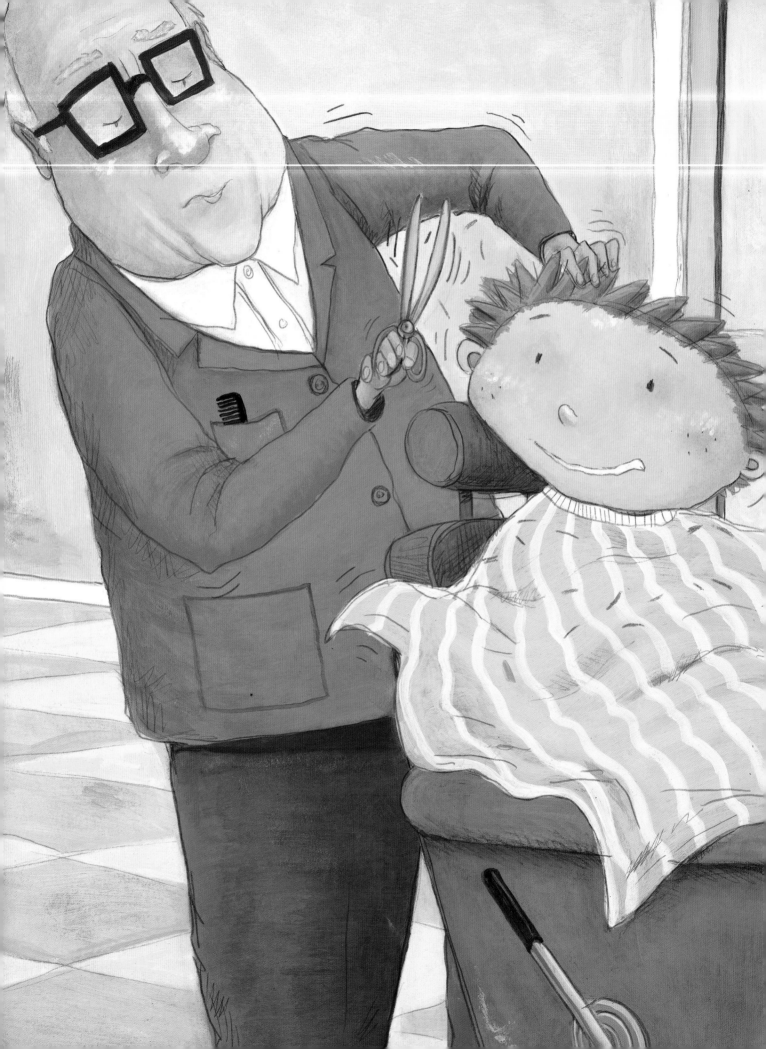

Why doesn't hair hurt
when you cut it?

Why can't I play with you?

Why are there so many numbers?

Why can't I have a tail?

Why?

Why can't I keep it in my room?

Why is it always your turn?

Why is it always my turn?

Why can't I come in?

Why do you care?

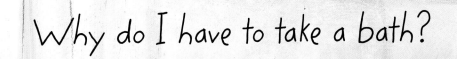

Why do I have to take a bath?

Why can't we read just one more book?

Why can't I jump on the bed?

Why do I have to go to
sleep if I'm not tired?

That's why.

Why? Copyright © 2010 by Richard Torrey. All rights reserved. Manufactured in China. No part of this book may be used or reproduced in any manner whatsoever without written permission except in the case of brief quotations embodied in critical articles and reviews. For information address HarperCollins Children's Books, a division of HarperCollins Publishers, 10 East 53rd Street, New York, NY 10022. www.harpercollinschildrens.com Library of Congress Cataloging-in-Publication Data Torrey, Rich. Why? / Richard Torrey. — 1st ed. p. cm. Summary: A young boy asks a lot of questions, including "Why does everyone think I ask too many questions?" ISBN 978-0-06-156170-2 (trade bdg.) [1. Curiosity—Fiction.] I. Title. PZ7.T64573Wh 2010 2009011749 [E]—dc22 CIP AC Typography by Dana Fritts. 10 11 12 13 14 LEO 10 9 8 7 6 5 4 3 2 1
❖ First Edition